Dear Parent:

Your child's love of reading starts here!

Every child learns to read in a different way and at his or her own speed. Some go back and forth between reading levels and read favorite books again and again. Others read through each level in order. You can help your young reader improve and become more confident by encouraging his or her own interests and abilities. From books your child reads with you to the first books he or she reads alone, there are I Can Read Books for every stage of reading:

SHARED READING
Basic language, word repetition, and whimsical illustrations, ideal for sharing with your emergent reader

BEGINNING READING
Short sentences, familiar words, and simple concepts for children eager to read on their own

READING WITH HELP
Engaging stories, longer sentences, and language play for developing readers

READING ALONE
Complex plots, challenging vocabulary, and high-interest topics for the independent reader

I Can Read Books have introduced children to the joy of reading since 1957. Featuring award-winning authors and illustrators and a fabulous cast of beloved characters, I Can Read Books set the standard for beginning readers.

A lifetime of discovery begins with the magical words **"I Can Read!"**

Visit www.icanread.com for information
on enriching your child's reading experience.

Library of Congress Control Number: 2020931683
ISBN 978-0-06-296336-9

Typography by Erica De Chavez

20 21 22 23 24   CWM   10 9 8 7 6 5 4 3 2   ❖   First Edition

I Can Read!

READING 3 ALONE

WW84™
WONDER WOMAN DC

DESTINED FOR GREATNESS

Adapted by Alexandra West
Illustrated by Walter Carzon

Wonder Woman created by
William Moulton Marston

Screenplay by:
Patty Jenkins
Geoff Johns
Dave Callahan

Story by:
Patty Jenkins
Geoff Johns

HARPER
An Imprint of HarperCollinsPublishers

On a magical, secret island

in the middle of the ocean,

people are celebrating.

Everyone is excited for the Amazon Games

The Amazon Games is an athletic competition,

a race with multiple events.

Only the fiercest warriors on the island

compete to win the Amazon Games.

Citizens gather to watch in a grand arena.

The queen of the Amazons leads
the Amazon Games.
Her name is Hippolyta.
Queen Hippolyta looks out into the crowd.
"Welcome, all," the queen says.
"The games today will determine
our strongest warrior."
Trumpets sound, alerting the crowd
that the games are about to begin.

The warriors begin to file into the arena.
The women are dressed in their competition gear.
They wear arm guards, sturdy sandals,
and headgear.

Princess Diana is competing in the Games.

There are six other warriors she must race.

But Diana is a little different.

She is the only child!

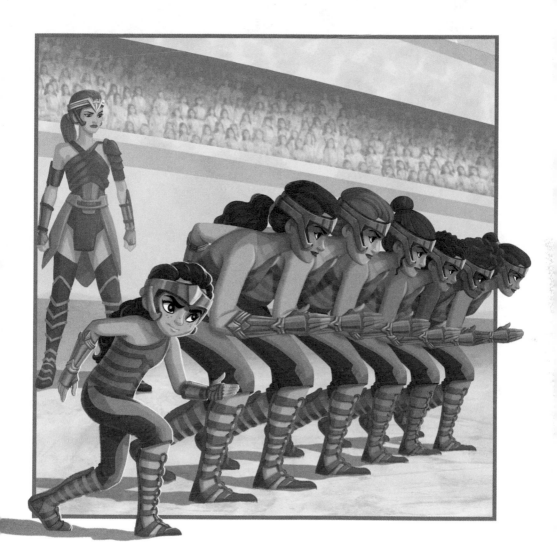

She is also the queen's daughter.

Diana wants to compete to prove

that she is as powerful a warrior as anyone.

She takes her place at the starting line.

One of the queen's guards bangs a giant gong.

The race has begun!

The warriors burst from the starting line, thinking of the challenge before them.

Diana keeps pace with the other warriors as they begin to speed through the course. She takes one last look over her shoulder, and then she bolts ahead.

The obstacle course contains tall platforms
and swinging wooden beams.
The course is designed so
only warriors with great strength,
balance, and agility will succeed.

Each warrior zips through the course
like it's no problem.
Diana uses her small size
to easily navigate the obstacles.

Diana is the first to reach the last beam
in the obstacle course.

She leaps off the end of the beam
and into the ocean below.

Diana lifts her head above water.

She sees horses waiting at the shoreline.

She swims ashore

and hops onto one of the stallions.

But the other warriors are close behind her.

Diana is in the lead!

Her heart pounds with excitement.

There is a path down the beach

that leads into the wilderness.

She rides up the path,

making sharp turns over rocky ground.

Diana is focused on only one thing.

She is focused on winning.

The other warriors are right behind her.

They steer their horses around the jagged rocks.

Each warrior has trained hard for this.

But Diana has trained hard, too.

Just then, Diana is distracted

and loses her balance.

She topples off her horse and loses her lead!

Diana refuses to give up.

She continues to run the race.

Though Diana loses the lead,
she finally makes it back to the arena.
There is one event left: the spear throw.
Diana must hurl her spear across the ring
and hit a bull's-eye.

Diana begins to sprint with her spear in hand.
Her heart is pounding.

But Diana loses fair and square.

Her aunt, Antiope, walks beside her.

Antiope tells Diana to keep practicing.

Queen Hippolyta walks over to console Diana,
who is sad.

She kisses Diana's head.

"Your time will come," she says.

"One day you will become
all of the things you dream of and more."

Although Diana didn't win the race,
she learned two important lessons.
You must never give up,
and becoming a great warrior takes time.

Luckily, she has some great teachers
to show her how.

Plus there's always next year!

Turn the page for more on
this moment from the film!

Meet The
AMAZONS

☆ PRINCESS DIANA ☆

An Amazonian princess, Diana is destined for greatness.
With the help of her mother and aunt, she is learning
what it takes to be a great Amazon warrior.

Ruler of the mystical island of Themyscira, Hippolyta values truth and justice above all else. These are the lessons she works hard to instill in her daughter.

QUEEN HIPPOLYTA

ANTIOPE

The most powerful warrior on Themyscira and the queen's sister, Antiope trains the Amazonians to be courageous and strong. She will eventually do the same with her niece, Diana.

Inside The ARENA

☆ CHEERING ON THE GAMES ☆

Thousands of citizens across Themyscira come to see the Amazon Games. They dress in their finest clothes and cheer for their favorite warriors.

☆ COMPETING IN THE GAMES ☆

The warriors who participate in the Amazon Games have been chosen for their strength and skill. Each warrior considers participating in the games a great honor.

The guards play an important role in the arena. They announce the beginning of the race and they keep the queen informed of the racers' progress.

☆ AMAZONIAN HORSES ☆

The arena is full of horses. From the queen's guards to the race itself, horses are a necessity if a warrior expects to win the Amazon Games. Having a fast horse means having a better chance of being crowned champion.

Though young Diana didn't win, the lessons she learned that day in the Amazon Games helped make her the person she is today. Not just a warrior, Diana has become all of the things she dreamed of and more. She has become Wonder Woman.